THE SCHOOL BOOK

TODD PARR

Megan Tingley Books

LITTLE, BROWN AND COMPANY

NEW YORK BOSTON

To all the teachers and librarians in the world

Also by Todd Parr

A complete list of Todd's books and more information can be found at toddparr.com.

About This Book

The illustrations for this book were created on a drawing tablet using an iMac, starting with bold black lines and dropping in color with Adobe Photoshop. This book was edited by Megan Tingley and Anna Prendella and designed by Jamie W. Yee. The production was supervised by Erika Breglia, and the production editor was Marisa Finkelstein. The text was set in Todd Parr's signature font.

It's time for school!

We get dressed.

We eat breakfast.

We pack our lunches.

We get our backpacks.

We all go to school.

We make everyone feel welcome.

We meet our teacher.

We have so much to do together.

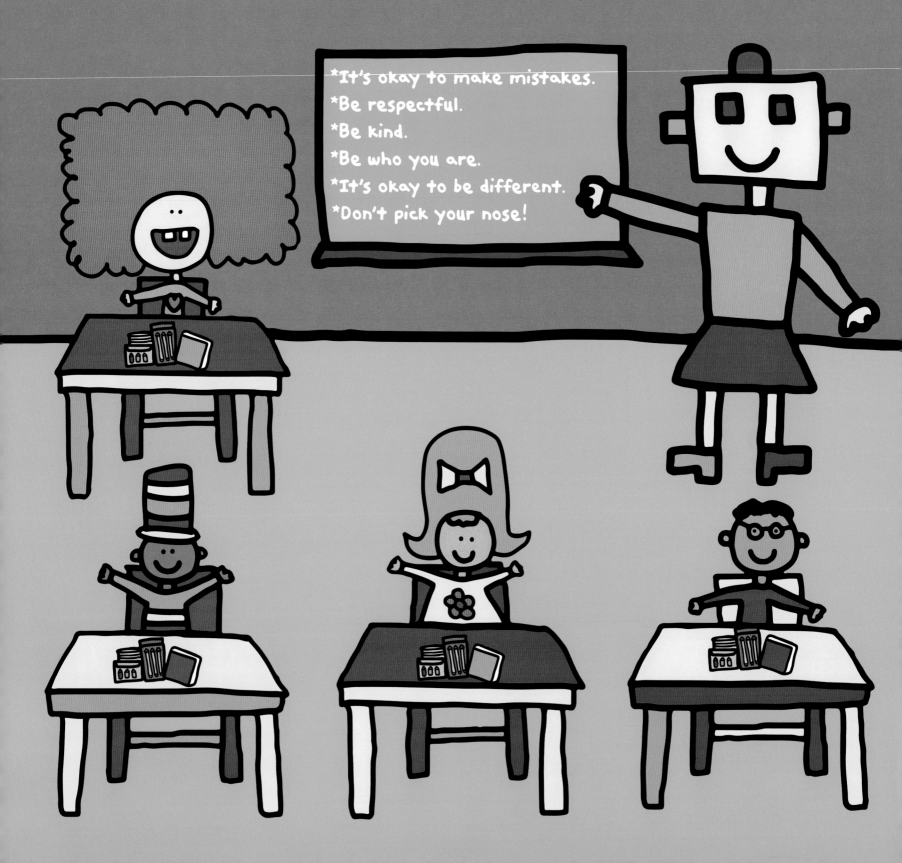

*It's okay to make mistakes.
*Be respectful.
*Be kind.
*Be who you are.
*It's okay to be different.
*Don't pick your nose!

We eat healthy snacks.

We take care of our pets.

We nap.

We visit the library.

We dance.

We play outside.

We eat lunch.

We have visitors.

If we get hurt, we get help.

We read lots of books.

We paint and draw.

We make things.

We water
our garden.

We exercise our bodies.

We relax our minds.

We share our stories.

There are lots of fun things to do at school. Always be kind. And don't pick your nose.

The End. Love, Todd